ON CAT MOUNTAIN

Françoise Richard
ILLUSTRATED BY Anne Buguet

G. P. Putnam's Sons

Some say the world is divided between those who love cats and those who do not. There are also those who love children and—thank goodness they are few—those whose hearts are simply too small to hold a child inside. But can you imagine a person so hard, so wicked as to love neither children nor cats?

Well, a long time ago, in a Japanese village far from here, there lived such a woman. Her voice was harsh, and her face was as sour as spoiled milk.

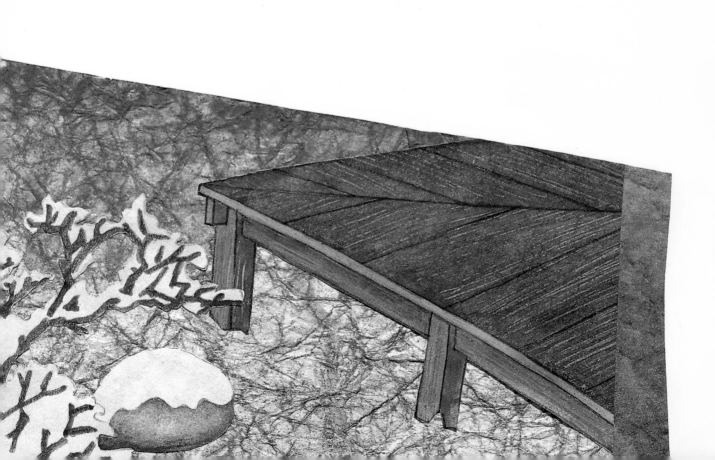

Sho was a quiet girl who lived as a servant in this nasty woman's house. Ever since Sho's parents died, she spent her days working hard, sharing her thoughts with no one.

But at night she poured out her dreams and hopes to the one friend she had—a sleek black cat whom she called Secret. No one knew about Secret, that Sho fed her fresh fish and stroked her warm fur. For if her mistress found out, her wrath would be terrible.

And one awful day it happened. The mistress found Sho scratching the cat's chin. *"How dare you bring that thing into my house!"* she screamed. Then she grabbed the startled cat by the scruff of the neck and began to shake her, until Secret howled and clawed the woman's hand.

When the mistress dropped her, Secret scampered off into the street and disappeared. "What have you to say for yourself?" the woman sneered.

"I am sorry, mistress," Sho whispered. But the words left a sharp taste in her mouth, like a bitter lemon.

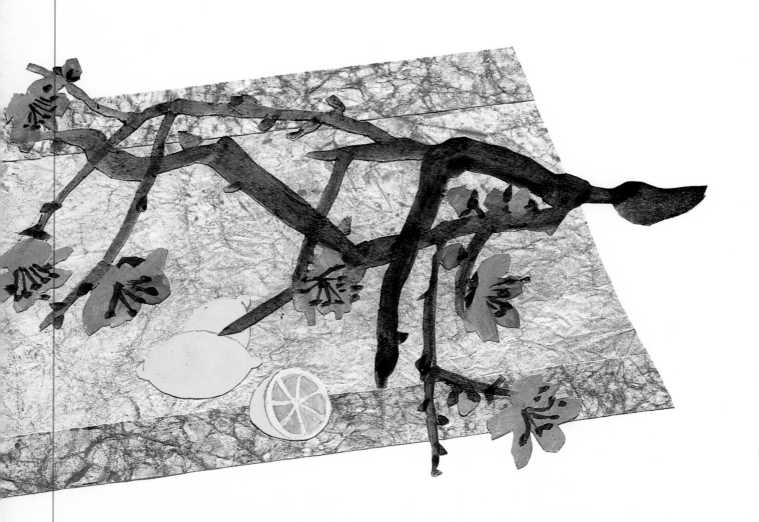

Time passed, and the cherry blossoms came and went, but Sho could not forget her friend. When it rained, she thought of her, dripping and cold. And at night she listened for Secret's purr.

Then one day the village buzzed with the news that a wise man, a fortune-teller, was coming. It was said he could answer any question. *Could he tell me where my Secret is?* Sho wondered. She squinted into the distance until she could see the fortune-teller's golden robes on the bridge.

Now the mistress had forbidden her servants to speak to the wise man. But when he arrived at the house, Sho could not help herself. When she thought no one was watching, she darted forward and whispered her question. The wise man fixed Sho with a steady gaze.

"What you have lost is more precious than anything your mistress owns," he said. "But you will find your Secret only on Cat Mountain. And that is a place from which no one has returned."

But the mistress had heard him. "More precious?" she cried. "Well, then, Sho will go to Cat Mountain and bring this secret back for me."

So with little more than a bundle of clothes, and a few flat cakes, Sho set off on the long, hard journey.

Step by step she made her way, wearing out her sandals on the sharp-stoned path. Whenever she asked for directions the people trembled. "We beg you not to go there," they said. "No one has ever returned from Cat Mountain!"

But Sho could not be turned aside. She followed the path into the hills, until her feet were bruised and her head spun. As the trees on the mountain grew darker and thicker, Sho thought she might have to give up.

Then suddenly, she parted a branch and walked into a clearing. There, bathed in golden sunlight, stood a group of houses with cheerful red roofs. Sho could smell dumplings in the steam from one window.

As she approached, a door opened and there appeared a young woman with strange amber eyes, wearing a brown and green kimono.

The woman's nose twitched, and she turned her head sharply toward Sho. "Yes?" she hissed. "What do you want?"

"I am looking for my little black cat. Have you seen her?" Sho asked quickly.

The woman licked her lips with a pointy pink tongue. "Mmmm. Don't you look delicious."

Sho took a step backward. But another woman appeared, with long black hair and a flowing red kimono.

"Don't be afraid," she said in a voice that purred soothingly. "You have come a long way. Rest. Eat a bit. Travelers are always welcome here." Just then a group of cats scampered past, and Sho saw one that reminded her of Secret. So she put aside her fears and followed the women inside.

There they treated Sho to a cool and fragrant bath, and gave her a fresh silk kimono. One woman brought her a tray filled with delicacies, and Sho bowed in gratitude. She had never received such attention!

After Sho had eaten, she wandered about the room. The walls were made of delicate paper screens, and from behind one of them she could hear the two women who had greeted her. Sho touched the panel and it moved slightly, so she could peer through the crack.

"I'm certain we would never eat a traveler who obviously loves cats!" said one.

"Oh, but she's such a tasty morsel..." said the other. Sho's skin went icy cold.

Sho heard a noise behind her, and whirled around, shutting the screens.

"Welcome to my home, Sho!" Before her stood a girl with the face of a cat. At first Sho was terrified, though the voice was strangely familiar. Then suddenly, with complete certainty, she knew. It was Secret! With shouts of joy the two friends rushed into each other's arms.

All day they sat together, talking and laughing, both of them speaking aloud what Sho alone could say before. They stopped only to sip from steaming cups of tea and to wrap themselves in quilted kimonos when the air grew cold.

Finally Sho asked Secret, "Tell me, dear friend, why did those women talk of eating me?"

"They are not women, don't you see? They are cats! They won't harm you as long as I am here." Secret's face grew long. "But you must leave soon, to be safe."

Secret sadly packed food and clothes for Sho's journey. Then she handed Sho a small embroidered bag. "We must say good-bye now, but take this as a reminder that you will always be in my heart. It will protect you on the journey, and once you are home it will gain you your freedom."

So Sho began the long hard journey back. In the thick, dark forest, wildcats growled fiercely. But they turned away when she held up the bag.

In one village Sho passed a man who had directed her before. "You—," he gasped, touching her arm to be sure she was not a ghost. "You came back!"

Whenever her legs grew heavy, Sho would think of Secret, and then she felt light as the wind.

Finally she arrived in the courtyard of her mistress's house. The other servants crowded around Sho and cheered as she told her story. When she opened the embroidered bag, a fortune in gold came tumbling out, and everyone clapped and danced.

Everyone except the mistress, that is.

The edges of the old woman's mouth stretched toward her chin, like cold
water dripping down a face of stone. "If that stupid little Sho can find a bag
of gold, then surely I can do better," she said, scowling. "After all, my rank
is infinitely superior."

So the very next day she set off for Cat Mountain. Servants carried her
high above the ground. A screen kept the sun from her eyes. Still she com-
plained. "Can't you walk any faster? Watch out for that bump! Ouch!"

When villagers tried to warn her of the danger, she spat on them and
shouted, "Out of my way!"

Her servants grew tired and bruised from the journey, and some got so
scared they fled for their lives, but eventually the caravan came to Cat
Mountain and to the clearing in the woods.

"This is mine!" shouted the mistress, dismissing her servants. Haughtily,
she approached the red-roofed houses.

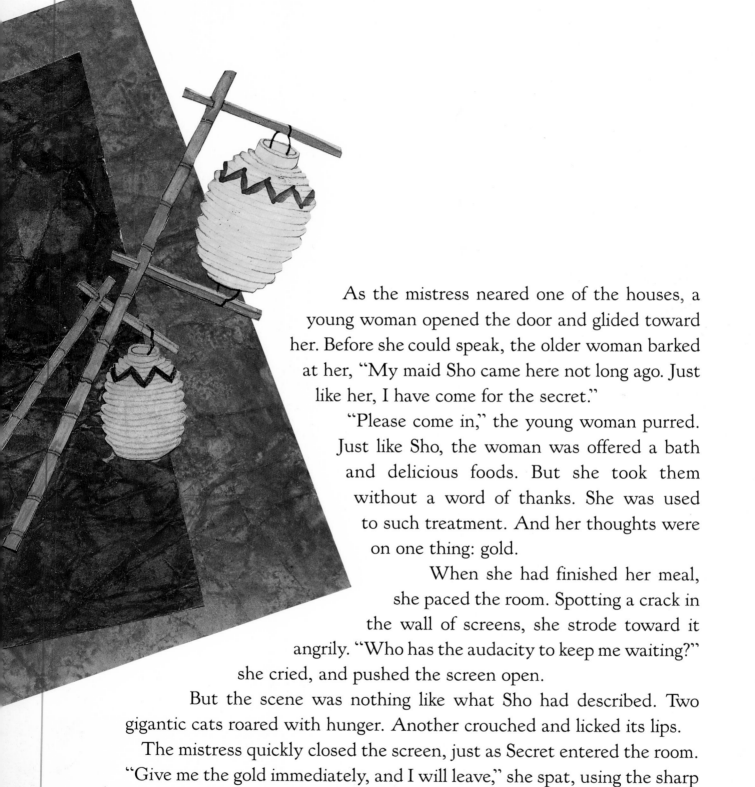

As the mistress neared one of the houses, a young woman opened the door and glided toward her. Before she could speak, the older woman barked at her, "My maid Sho came here not long ago. Just like her, I have come for the secret."

"Please come in," the young woman purred. Just like Sho, the woman was offered a bath and delicious foods. But she took them without a word of thanks. She was used to such treatment. And her thoughts were on one thing: gold.

When she had finished her meal, she paced the room. Spotting a crack in the wall of screens, she strode toward it angrily. "Who has the audacity to keep me waiting?" she cried, and pushed the screen open.

But the scene was nothing like what Sho had described. Two gigantic cats roared with hunger. Another crouched and licked its lips.

The mistress quickly closed the screen, just as Secret entered the room. "Give me the gold immediately, and I will leave," she spat, using the sharp tone of voice her servants knew only too well.

But Secret let out a strident call. And all at once the screens flew open. Wildcats entered from every side and devoured the wicked woman on the spot.

In all of Japan, not a soul mourned her. As for Sho, she opened a little shop in her village and led a long and honorable life. And whenever she saw a stray cat she would stop and stroke behind its ears. Then she would feed it some fish or a bowl of milk and send it on its way with a gift. "Go find Cat Mountain," she'd whisper. "Give my dear Secret a flower from her friend."

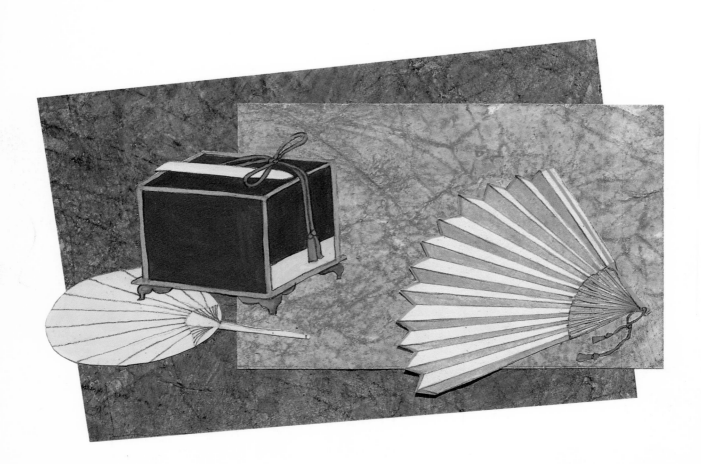

English-language adaptation by Arthur A. Levine
English-language adaptation copyright © 1994 by G. P. Putnam's Sons
Illustrations copyright © 1993 by Anne Buguet
Original-edition text copyright © 1993 by Françoise Richard
All rights reserved. This book, or parts thereof, may not be reproduced
in any form without permission in writing from the publisher.
First American edition published in 1994 by G. P. Putnam's Sons,
a division of The Putnam & Grosset Group, 200 Madison Avenue,
New York, NY 10016. G. P. Putnam's Sons, Reg. U.S. Pat. & Tm. Off.
Originally published in French in 1993 by Albin Michel
Jeunesse, Paris, under the title *La Montagne aux chats*.
Published simultaneously in Canada.
Printed in Hong Kong by South China Printing Co. (1988) Ltd.
Designed by Colleen Flis. Text set in Kennerley.

Library of Congress Cataloging-in-Publication Data
Levine, Arthur A., 1962-   On Cat Mountain / written by Françoise Richard;
adapted by Arthur A. Levine; illustrated by Anne Buguet. — 1st American ed.   p.   cm.
Rev. translation of: La Montagne aux Chats / Françoise Richard. 1993.
Summary: A young girl goes on a long and difficult journey in search of
the cat that had been her friend and when she returns with treasure,
her harsh mistress makes the same journey with very different results.
[1. Folklore—Japan. 2. Cats—Folklore.] I. Richard, Françoise,
1951-   Montagne aux Chats. II. Buguet, Anne, ill. III. Title.
PZ8.1.L4370n 1994   398.24`52974428—dc20 93-11408 CIP AC

ISBN 0-399-22608-7
1 3 5 7 9 10 8 6 4 2
First American Edition